Too Many
Valentines

For the children of
St. Hilda's and St. Hugh's School
—Margaret McNamara

First Aladdin Paperbacks edition January 2003

Text copyright © 2003 by Simon & Schuster
Illustrations copyright © 2003 by Mike Gordon

ALADDIN PAPERBACKS
An imprint of Simon & Schuster
Children's Publishing Division
1230 Avenue of the Americas
New York, NY 10020

The text for this book was set in CentSchbook BT.
Book design by Sammy Yuen Jr.

Printed in the United States of America
6 8 10 9 7

Library of Congress Cataloging-in-Publication Data
McNamara, Margaret.
Too many valentines / by Margaret McNamara ; illustrated by Mike Gordon.
p. cm. — (Robin Hill School)
Summary: When Neil tells his classmates that he does not want any more
valentines, especially pink or frilly ones, the class comes up with a good idea.
ISBN 0-689-85537-0 (pbk.) — ISBN 0-689-85538-9 (lib. bdg.)
0410 LAK
[1. Valentine's Day—Fiction. 2. Schools—Fiction.] I. Gordon, Mike,
ill. II. Title.
PZ7.M232518 To 2003
[E]—dc21
2002008833

Robin Hill School

Too Many Valentines

Written by Margaret McNamara
Illustrated by Mike Gordon

Ready-to-Read
Aladdin Paperbacks
New York   London   Toronto   Sydney   Singapore

"It is almost Valentine's Day,"
said Mrs. Connor.
"Today we will make cards."

All the children
at Robin Hill School
loved Valentine's Day.

All the children
except Neil.

"Valentines are frilly!
Valentines are pink!"
he said.

"I get too many valentines.
I do not want any more."

"Are you sure?"
asked Mrs. Connor.
"Yes, I am sure," said Neil.
"Very, very sure."
And that was that.

On Valentine's Day,
Katie gave Emma
a frilly valentine.

James gave Hannah
a pink valentine.

But nobody
gave a valentine
to Neil.

Mrs. Connor asked him,
"Is it all right
that you did not get
any valentines?"

"Yes," said Neil.

"It is great."

But inside,
Neil did not feel great
at all.

On the playground
all the children
looked at their valentines.

Neil looked at the swings.

In the halls
all the children
read their
valentines.

Neil read a book.

On the school bus
all the children
talked about their valentines.

Neil talked about
his soccer team.
But nobody listened.

When Neil got home
his sister said,
"Neil, this card
came for you."

Neil opened the envelope.

Inside was a valentine.
It was not frilly.
It was not pink.

Every first grader
in Neil's class
signed the card.

We thought you
would be SAD
if there was no
valentine
for you!

Hannah

Michael

Reza   Emma

Ayanan

James   Katie

Eigen

Mia

Griffin

The next day
Mrs. Connor asked,
"Did you get too
many valentines,
Neil?"

"No," said Neil.
"I did not get
   too many valentines.
   I got just one valentine.
   And I feel great."

This time, he did.